25^P

Ella

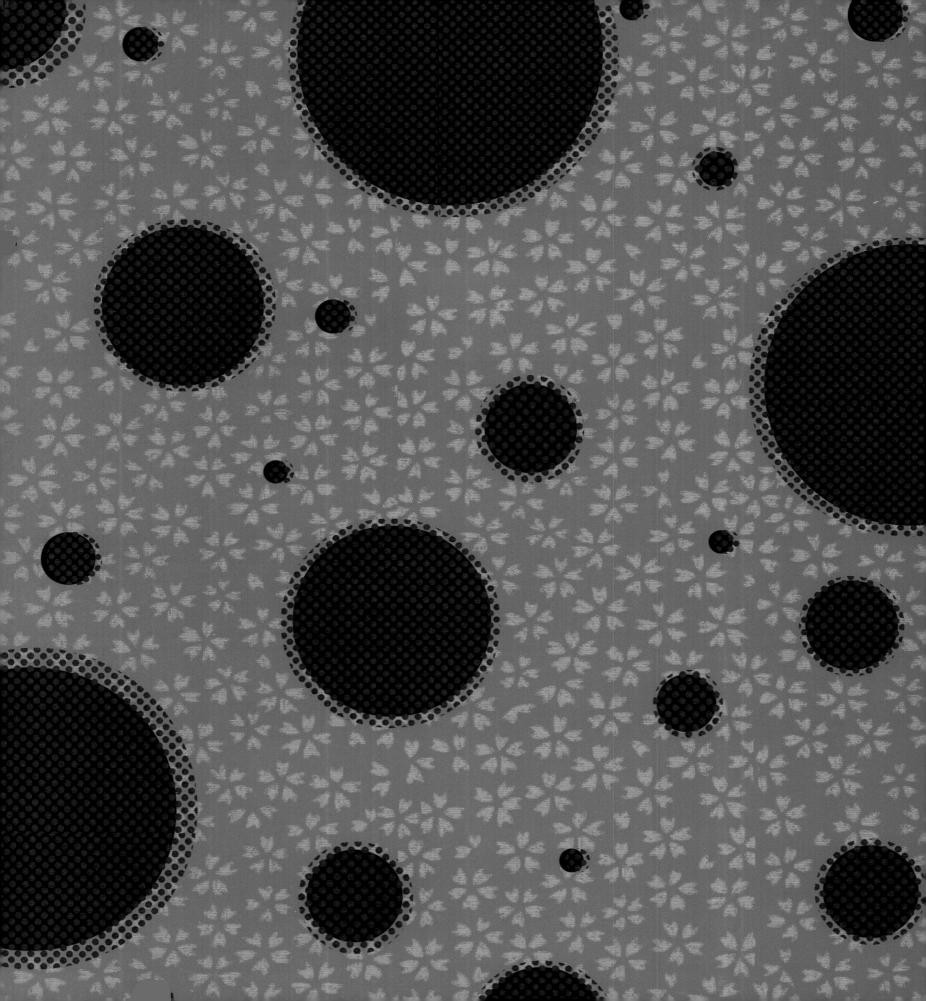

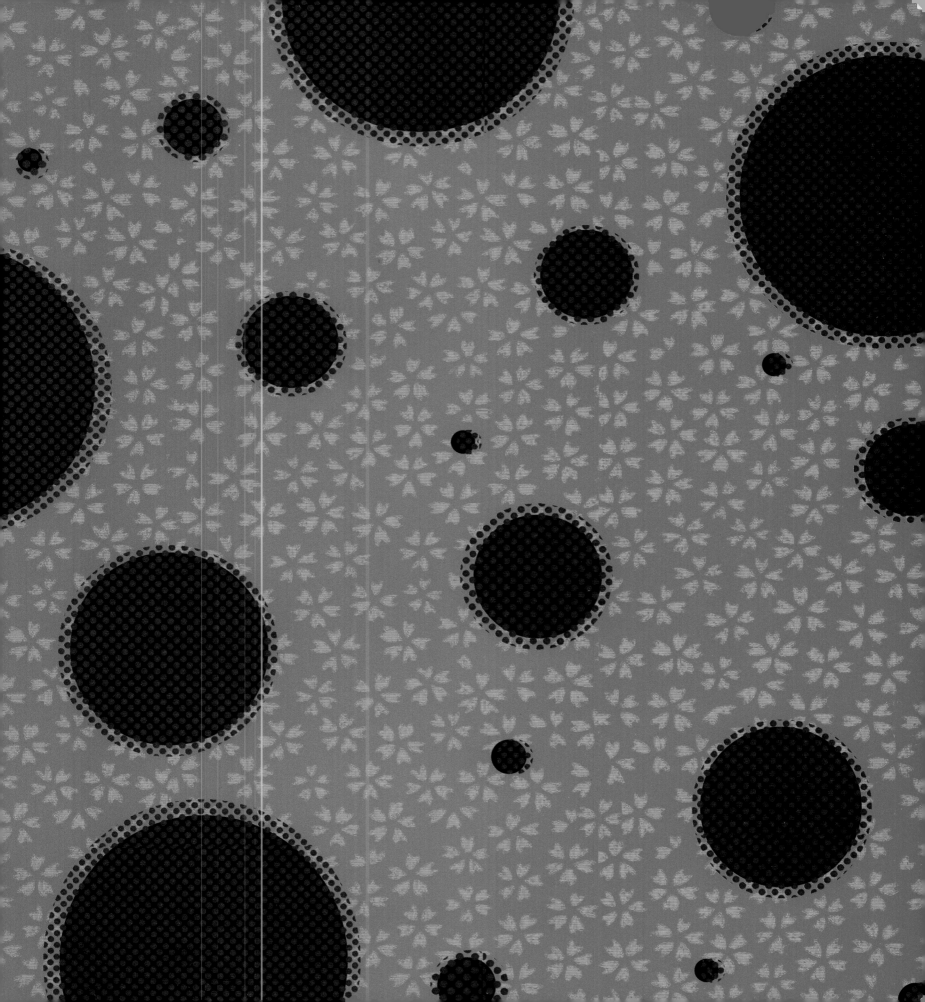

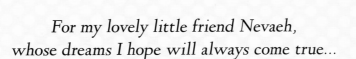

For my lovely little friend Nevaeh,
whose dreams I hope will always come true...
x
A.T.S.

First published in 2012 by Scholastic Children's Books
Euston House, 24 Eversholt Street
London NW1 1DB
a division of Scholastic Ltd
www.scholastic.co.uk
London ~ New York ~ Toronto ~ Sydney ~ Auckland
Mexico City ~ New Delhi ~ Hong Kong

HB 978 1407 10963 3
PB 978 1407 10964 0

11 13 15 17 19 20 18 16 14 12

Once upon a time,
there was a ladybird called Ella.

Ella was always tired because she was forever slaving away after her spoilt stepsisters, Belladonna and Ivy.

She dusted their wings, she picked up their shoes...

...and she scrubbed their pillowcases after they had eaten jam sandwiches in bed.

And the wasp sisters **never**, ever said thank you.

"Don't worry, honey," hummed Ella's friend, Ms Buzzbottom. "One day your life will change forever!"

At that very moment in Paris, a famous artist named Pierre was sighing.

He didn't know what to paint.

Suddenly, an idea pinged into his head.
He would throw a Grand Bug Ball.
That was sure to inspire him!

A few days later, an
envelope arrived for the
wasp sisters...

Belladonna and Ivy were all of a flutter, as both secretly hoped that handsome Pierre would fall in **love** with them.

"You must come too..."
they snapped at Ella,

"**...to carry our bags.**"

Paris was enchanting, but the wasp sisters didn't care. They needed their beauty sleep.

Ella slipped out to explore. She was zipping down the boulevard when she bumped into a handsome spider. He was knocked off his feet and got his legs in a tangle.

He looked into Ella's big eyes as she helped him up.

"Thank you," he said, and he kissed her hands. All four of them.

Ella blushed and scuttled back to her hotel, leaving the handsome spider wondering who this exquisite creature was.

Back at the hotel, Ella helped squeeeeeeze her stepsisters into their party dresses before they buzzed off to the ball.

Ella sighed.
How she would love to go!

Just then there came a loud

buzzing

noise from outside the window. On the balcony was Ella's very own invitation to the ball – and a big box with her name on it!

The writing looked just like Ms Buzzbottom's...

Inside the box was a beautiful ball gown and a pair of glittery glasses.

Dear Ella

You are invited to the
Grand Bug Ball
at
The Chandelier Café in Paris
On Valentine's Day

Wear your sparkliest party clothes, and be ready to dance the night away.

Love from
Pierre
x

When Ella arrived at the ball, she turned
everyone's heads.

They had never seen such a **stunning** bug.

Pierre was entranced with the lovely spotty
stranger and danced with her all night long.

"Who is that silly creature
in those silly specs?" spat
Belladonna and Ivy.
"Pierre should be dancing
with us, not her!"

The evening was

★ ★ ★ ★ ★

★ magical. ★

★ ★ ★ ★ ★

But all too soon it was **midnight** and Ella had to get back to the hotel before her stepsisters. She quickly said goodbye and left.

"**Wait!**" cried Pierre, "I don't even know your name!"

But Ella had gone.

The next morning Pierre tried to paint a picture of the mysterious stranger, but he just couldn't get it right.

"I must see her again!" he thought.

Then, as he clutched her sparkly specs, an idea shot into his head...

There was great excitement all over Paris
as the news was announced.

Pierre was searching for the spotty stranger,
and he wanted all the bugs in Paris to come
and try on the sparkly spectacles.

Belladonna and Ivy set off.

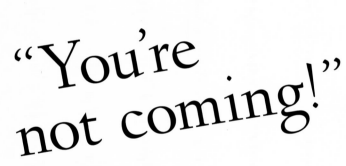

"You're not coming!"

they hissed at Ella.

"Yes I am!" she whispered.

A long line wiggled outside Pierre's studio.
Pierre handed the glasses to each lady in turn.

Belladonna and Ivy looked **ridiculous**.

Pierre was about to give up when he spotted Ella.

"I'm so happy
we keep bumping
into each other!" he grinned.

Even in her ordinary glasses, Ella
looked more beautiful to him than any
bug in Paris.

He had found the bug he was looking for.

Pierre started on a painting of Ella immediately.

It was a **spectacular** success.
Everyone in Paris went dotty
over Ella's spots...

...and she and Pierre lived

happily
ever after.

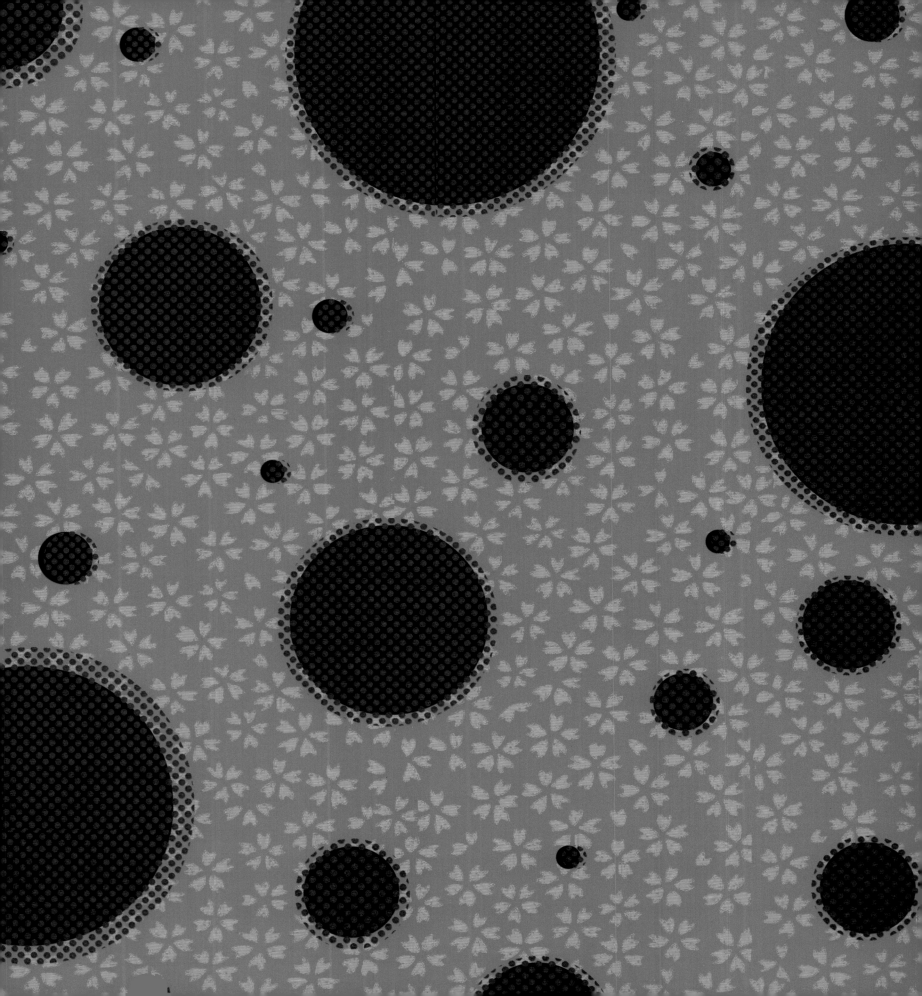

The End

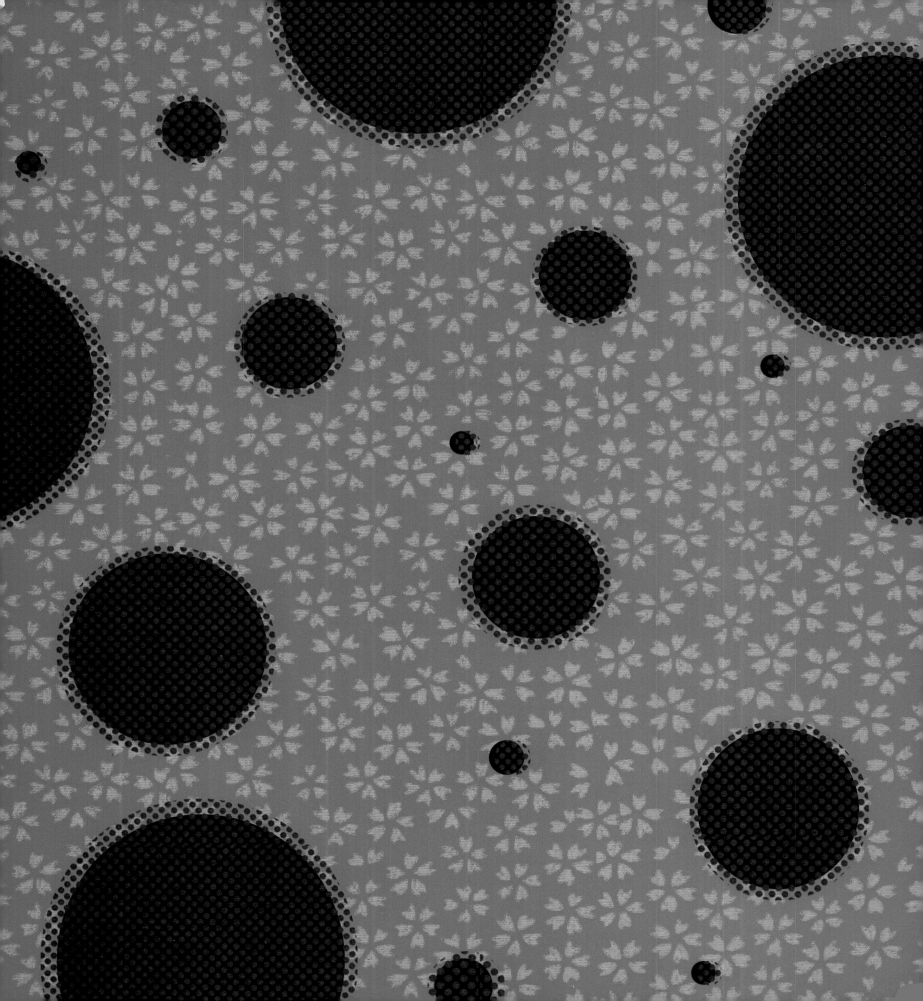